Brushing Mom's Hair

Brushing Mom's Hair

ANDREA CHENG

ILLUSTRATIONS BY
NICOLE WONG

WORDSONG
Honesdale, Pennsylvania

Also by Andrea Cheng

Marika
Honeysuckle House
The Lace Dowry
Tire Mountain
Eclipse
Where the Steps Were
The Bear Makers

Library of Congress Cataloging-in-Publication Data

Cheng, Andrea.
Brushing Mom's hair / Andrea Cheng ; illustrations by Nicole Wong.
— 1st ed.
p. cm.
Summary: A fourteen-year-old girl, whose mother's breast cancer
diagnosis and treatment have affected every aspect of their lives,
finds release in ballet and art classes.
ISBN 978-1-59078-599-7 (hardcover : alk. paper)
[1. Novels in verse. 2. Cancer—Fiction. 3. Sick—Fiction.
4. Mothers and daughters—Fiction. 5. Schools—Fiction.
6. Ballet—Fiction. 7. Handicraft—Fiction.]
I. Wong, Nicole (Nicole E.), ill. II. Title.
PZ7.5.C44Bru 2009
[Fic]—dc22
2009021965

WORDSONG
An Imprint of Boyds Mills Press, Inc.
815 Church Street
Honesdale, Pennsylvania 18431

10 9 8 7 6 5 4 3 2

To Nicholas, Jane, and Ann

—A.C.

In memory of Marie and Fran

—N.W.

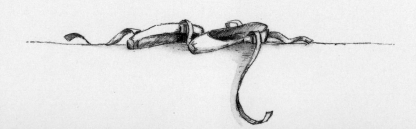

Ballet

We stretch,
thin arms
touching toes.
Linda says,
Can you believe
my mom's friend
had one of her breasts
cut off?
Becky covers her mouth
with her hand.
Really?
I look at them
in the mirror,
eyebrows raised,
eyes open
wide.
I bend
and touch my forehead
to my knee.
I don't say,
My mom
had both her breasts cut off
and now she has stitches
covered by bandages
where they were.

Tubes

Massage the tubes
three times a day,
the directions say.
Mom takes the instructions
into the bathroom.
My sister Jane
follows her in.
I hear their voices—
Like this,
that's right,
squeeze here.
Rubber tubes
with bulbs attached,
like turkey basters.
I wait
outside the door.

Marsupial

Marsupials,
animals that carry
their babies in pouches,
kangaroos
and wallabies
and koala bears.
In the dark mornings
when Nick and Jane
had left for school,
Mom used to wrap me
in her terry-cloth robe
and we'd sit,
Mama Kangaroo and Baby One.
Now she has a pouch
of white terry cloth
to hold the bulbs
attached to the tubes.
It's called
a marsupial.

The Doorknob

The door is stuck.
I pull so hard,
the knob comes out
in my hand.
Now there is a hole
where the knob was.
The rod is stripped
and nobody has time
to get a new one.
Dad puts rope
through the hole
and wraps it
with duct tape.
The door
doesn't lock.
That's okay.
Mom is always home.

Flowers

Flowers in vases
and plants in wicker pots
with fake moss.
The doorbell rings
every minute.
*Nice doorknob
you got there,*
a delivery man says.
*My mom
has breast cancer,*
I say.
He looks down.
I can tell him
but I can't tell
the girls at ballet.

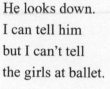

School

Teachers smile,
the ones I like
and the ones I don't.
How's your mom?
How does everyone know
already?
I sit in the art room
and paint wax
onto the fabric,
a thin girl
with arms raised,
turning.
Ms. Smith doesn't say,
How's your mom?
She says,
Have you decided
on a color
for the dye?
Stay as long as you want.
I'm not leaving
for a while.

Chili

Chili with black beans,
chili with red beans,
vegetarian chili
spicy or mild.
So nice of everyone.
Thank you
so very much.
Unfortunately,
I hate beans.

Sorry

Miss Jones says,
*So sorry
your mom is sick.*
She brings us a whole box
of chocolate buckeyes.
Mom invites her in
and she tells us about her aunt
who had cancer.
Is she doing better now?
Mom asks.
*My aunt?
Oh, she died
last year.*

New Chair

When I had pneumonia
we sat,
me and Mom,
in the rocking chair
for two days
until I slid
onto the carpet
and built a tower
with blocks.
Now my aunt
got us a new chair,
maroon
with blue dots.
The old rocking chair
is in the basement.
I sit there
and do my homework
while Mom sleeps
in the new chair.

Biology Homework

A brown cow and a white bull,
how will their babies
turn out?
Some brown, some white,
some spotted.
The washing machine
stops churning our clothes.
I hang the jeans
on the line
by the furnace,
my short ones
and Jane's long.
I wonder
which one of us
has the cancer gene.

Dance

I leap
across the studio floor,
springs in my feet,
jump, spin, land wrong.
I go to the bathroom
and wrap my ankle
with elastic
so nobody
can see it
swell.

Exercises

Mom's shoulder froze.
Why didn't they tell her
to move it more?
Now she has to
walk her arm
up the wall.
Her eyes are shut,
lips pressed tight.
I wish I could
stay in the studio
and dance forever
even if my ankle
hurts.

Birthday

Fifteen,
no driver's license yet,
but still.
Grams bakes apple cake.
The cousins come.
I get nice pens,
a sweater,
and a book
of quotations.
Mom is asleep
in the new chair.
She wakes up
and gives me a package—
a new leotard,
the kind I like,
with straps that cross,
extra small,
perfect.

Nick

Nick calls
from California.
–Happy birthday.
–Thanks.
–How's Mom?
–Pretty good.
She's asleep.
–That's good.
Did you get the package?
–Not yet.
–Maybe tomorrow.
I better go,
the cafeteria's
about to close.
–Okay.
–Say hi to everyone.
–Okay.
–Happy birthday.
–Thanks.
Nick?
I forgot to tell him
the doorknob broke.
He better come home
and fix it.

Night

It's midnight
but I can't sleep
so I turn on the light
and open my new book
to the middle.
Don't sweat the small stuff
and it's all small stuff.
Even cancer?

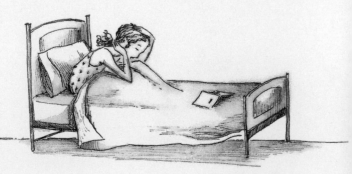

Healing

No more marsupials,
no more stitches,
no more tubes,
no more breasts,
just scars,
nothing.

After School

Me and Suzanne
take the bus
to get ice cream—
so what if it's winter?
She tells me about Adam,
how he kissed her
after riding practice
in the barn.
We laugh
behind ice-cream cones.
Is he your boyfriend?
She shrugs.
He hardly talks to me.

Present

The package
could have walked,
it took so long.
Inside
is a rolled-up T-shirt,
black,
extra small.
National Day of Silence
April 15
I am silencing myself
in solidarity
with those who are silenced
by others
in white print.
I try it on
with my favorite jeans.
In front of the mirror,
développé,
arabesque,
sauté.
I can't wait
to show Suzanne.
But I talked
on April 15,
so is it still okay
to wear the shirt?
I hold it to my face
and smell my brother.

Chemo

Chemo 1,
Chemo 2,
Chemo 3,
Chemo 4,
Chemo 5,
Chemo 6,
every three weeks,
December seventeenth
to April second.
I mark each one
in a different color
on the calendar.
The last one
is fluorescent purple.
I make a smiley face
with curly hair
to mark the end
even though Mom will be bald
by then.

Chemo 1

I stay with Ms. Smith
at lunch
and use her phone.
—How's Mom?
—She's fine,
asleep.
Dad's voice is hoarse.
—Are you sure
she's okay?
—I'm sure.
I dip
my fabric
in red dye
and let it soak.
Tomorrow I'll iron out
the wax.
I wish I didn't have
to go to English
every single day.
I'd much rather
make a batik
and smell the wax and vinegar
and eat popcorn with Ms. Smith
but the bell's already
ringing.

Water

Mom's supposed to drink
eighty ounces a day
for three days.
I make a bar graph
on the computer
marked off by eights.
You better drink more.
The doctor said.
Mom gulps
one more cup.
Fifty-six ounces to go
and it's already
five o'clock.
What if
she doesn't make it
to eighty?
Jane says, *Leave her alone,*
she's tired.
Why'd I make the graph then?

Leg Warmers

Grams casts on
twenty stitches
and shows me how to knit
on four needles
so there's no seam,
perfect for leg warmers,
green and brown
striped.
We sit in the living room
and knit together
and listen to the news.
Grams is making a white chemo hat
that looks pink
in the sunset.

Haircut

Mom cuts her hair
short like my brother's.
It will fall out anyway,
she says.
Better to have less
than more.
But maybe
there's a chance
it won't.

Scarves

My cousin and I
cut and hem
and fringe the ends.
Beautiful scarves,
yellow and blue and green.
I dance and twirl them
in front of the mirror.
My cousin picks one up
and throws it high.
We forget
they are for Mom's head
when it's bald
and we laugh.

Hats

Mom wears
the hats Grams made
because they won't slip off
like scarves
and leave her naked
at the grocery store.

Snow

So quiet.
The snow is falling
fast.
Mom makes a snowball
and throws it at me
and I throw one back.
We get hot.
Mom takes off
the white hat.
Snow lands
on her bald head
and melts.

Snow Day

Jane whispers
in the dark,
It's a snow day!
We tiptoe down,
put on snow pants
that are much too short,
and get the saucers
with fall leaves still stuck
in spiderwebs.
We push each other
down the hill
that used to seem big,
spinning,
laughing,
dizzy,
wet.

My stomach growls.
We go home
and stamp off our boots
on the porch.
Then I remember
that Mom has cancer.

The Nutcracker

I'm a mouse
in the battle
and a snowflake
in Snow.
I can't wait
to show Mom,
but if her white count
is too low
she can't come,
I know.
I scan the crowd.
There's Ms. Smith
in back
and Suzanne
and Grams
and Jane
and Dad
and no scarf, no hat, just Mom.

Germs

Week three
the white count is so low,
even a cold
would be serious.
I squirt hand cleaner
on every single person
who comes to our house
and wash all the apples
and oranges
twice.
Jane says,
*You're driving me crazy
with all that cleaning,*
but what's she going to do
if Mom catches a cold,
I'd like to know.

Clay

Slice and throw,
knead those air bubbles
out.
Center the mound,
draw it up,
a nice wide bowl
for soup
or rice.
I slice it off the wheel
and throw a mug
for Nick.
By the time the chemo ends
we'll have a whole set.

Every day
Jane sits on the couch
and reads Mom poems.
She's sleeping,
I say.
I know,
but maybe she hears
something.
I sit on the floor
and do my math.
Mom whispers,
Can you please
read that one about the turtle
again?

Trim

*How much
do you want off?*
the lady asks
Suzanne.
Suzanne looks at me.
An inch?
I nod.
Layers?
Sure.
I pull my curls back
and wish I had straight hair
like Suzanne.
I should shave my head
to match Mom's
and donate the curls
to Locks of Love,
but I'm not that brave,
not brave at all.

Dress

Me and Jane
plan my dress,
brown
to match my skin,
with a ruffle
on the bottom.
Everything looks cute
on you,
she says.
I smile
in the dark.
But what if
nobody asks me
to dance?

Melting

Snow is melting, sun is strong.
Mom sits by the wall
where there is no wind
and feels the warm bricks
of our house
on her back.
She takes off her hat.
The whole world can see
no hair,
no eyebrows,
no eyelashes.
A policeman pulls over.
Everything all right?
he asks.

Pretty Good Day

We go to the indoor pool.
The old ladies
know Mom.
—How are you feeling
today?
—Pretty good.
—This is your daughter?
Nice to meet you.
We all change
in the big room.
I don't care
that my underwear
comes up too high
and my breasts
are small.
One lady has
a hunched back.
Her breasts sag.
Mom looks sleek
and fit
and happy.

Earrings

I help Dad
pick out dangles,
silver
with amber beads.
They look so nice
with Mom's long neck.
She puts them on
and we take a walk
around the block.
Yellow crocuses are blooming
on the corner.
Mom's eyes
get teary
when she sees them.

Plates

I throw a whole set
of plates
to match the bowls
and set them on the shelf
to dry.
Mom always wanted
nice dishes.
Now finally
her dream will come true.

Chemo 4

Mom passes out
on the floor.
The doctor says drink.
She did
but she threw up.
Now she's asleep.
Jane reads poems
of trees in winter.
Her voice is soft.
The sun is setting.
Dad sits on the edge of the sofa,
listening.
The phone rings.
—How's Mom?
—Asleep.
—That's good.
—How's school going?
—Okay.
I miss you guys.
I don't tell Nick
that Mom passed out.
He has no idea.

Batik

Four small batiks,
dancers
in wax,
dancers
in dye,
dancers
for Mom.

Food

Everyone says
I'm too thin.
I eat a lot
but can't they see
I have to dance
every single day?
The pianist
moves his fingers
fast
over the keys.
I jump
to make the lines
I want,
clean and straight.
The music fills me up
more than chili
or pie
or popcorn.

Goodwill

I run my hand
down the rack,
silk and cotton,
linen and wool.
I hold up a dress.
Suzanne smiles.
Try it on, I say.
It would be too big for me,
but it fits her
perfect.
We look
for three hours
but the only dress
that fits me
is a girl's twelve
with purple flowers
on the collar.
*What about the brown one
you sewed?*
I shrug.
I might not go to the dance
at all.
I find a boy's jean jacket
for two dollars.
Then we go across the street
to get a hamburger
but I can only eat
a little.

Cake

Mom's friend brings us cake
but her eyes are sad.
Her new grandson
has a problem,
a genetic defect
they never knew he had,
a hole in his heart,
a brain too small.
But she brought us cake.

English

Why can't we just read a book?
Why do we have to figure out
what symbolizes what?
I stare at
the blank computer screen.
Then I make Mom
a new background,
a whole field
of crocuses.

March

Suzanne says
she's done with boys.
They're dumb,
they're immature,
they have nothing
to say.
I don't know.
A boy in my art class
said his mom
had a brain tumor.
They took it out
and now she's learning how to write
again.

The Dance

I take off my shoes
and do line dances.
Four boys in a row
ask Suzanne to dance.
I go into the bathroom
and when I come back
Suzanne and this boy
she just met
are making out
behind the door.
I wish
I never made the dress.
I wish I was standing
at the bar,
every muscle
controlled,
the tilt of my head,
the turn of my hand,
just right.
Instead
I stand by the door
and wait.

April 2

I want to celebrate
the last chemo
but Mom is sleeping.
She'll sleep for three days,
then no more chemo
ever,
ever.
Grams makes dinner,
food I like,
rice and chicken,
apple cake,
no chili,
no beans.
After dinner
I bring Mom
a glass of water.
Mom,
you still have to drink,
remember?
She looks at me
like *Leave me alone.*
I throw the graph
into the garbage.

Forgiveness

Some lady told Mom
you get cancer
if you don't forgive people
and now
I can't forgive
that lady.

Bowls

Two bowls crack
in the kiln
and one has a dent
on the side,
but I like the glaze,
brown with green specks,
like Mom's eyes.
I'll glaze the plates
to match.

Nobody's Home

Mom?
No answer.
Mom?
My stomach flips.
She's at the hospital,
she passed out
again.
I call Grams.
No answer.
I call Dad.
Please leave a message
at the beep,
but I don't.
Everyone's
at the hospital
except me.
I look up the street.
Some daffodils are open,
some are shut.
Where is Mom?

Jane walks in.
Mom went back to work,
remember?

Milk Shake

*Add ice cream
and a banana,
make it thick,
drink it all.*
Can't Mom stop bugging me
to eat?
*I'm full,
okay?*
My voice is sharp.
Her eyes
tear up.
Mom's not like
she used to be.

Waiting

Dad says
you don't get over things
that quick.
Maybe
you don't get over them
ever.

I'm tired of waiting
for chemo
every three weeks,
for hair
to fall out
and grow back,
for my ankle to heal,
for my brother
to come home,
for my old mom.

Cleaning

Mom is scrubbing
the kitchen floor.
My mother
is cleaning
again!
I put a sponge
in the bucket
and make a big wet circle
on the floor
with two eyes
and a smile.
Mom's head
is near my face.
Hey, could that be hair
growing back?

Toothbrush

I ride to Walgreens
on my bike
and buy a pink toothbrush.
Then I brush Mom's fuzz
up and down and all around.
It's black, Mom,
and thick.
Here, feel this,
curly and soft
like a baby's,
fresh and new.
The sun is shining
on the wood floor.
I push away from the chair
and dance.